When I am Quiet on Maui

by Judi Riley

Hawaii is home to some of the most rare and endangered animals in the world.
Open your senses and drift into a world of make-believe encounters with some unusual animal friends.
But remember to tell your keiki (kay-key, child) that in real life, it is important to admire wildlife from afar.

For: Boo

Look for more Tiki Tales:

When I am Quiet on Kauai

When I am Quiet on Oahu

When I am Quiet on the Big Island

©2002

Published by Tiki Tales

P.O. Box 1194, Haiku, Hi 96708

www.tikitales.com

jamriley@hawaii.rr.com

ISBN 0-9740582-0-3

Printed and Bound in China

When you are quiet,
what do you hear?

When you are still,
what do you feel?

When I am quiet
on Mt. Haleakala soon after sunrise,
I hear the willowy wind
woooo—sh across the crater floor.

Haleakala (*Hah-lay-ah-kah-la*) — "house of the sun" — Maui's dormant volcano

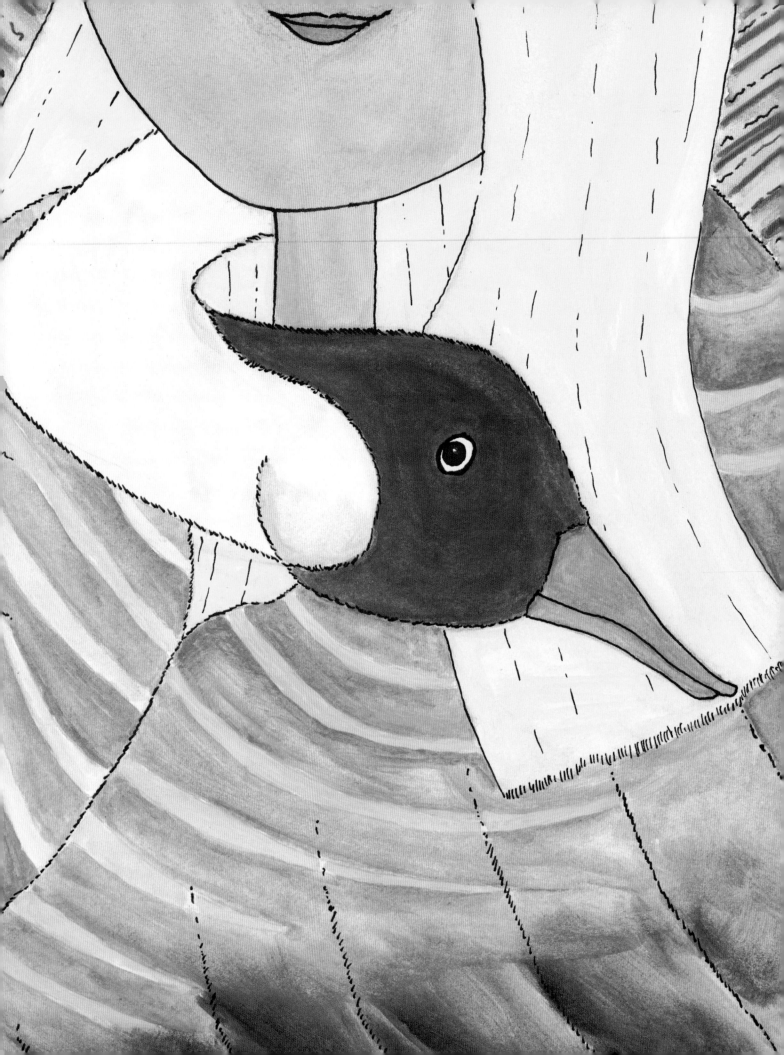

When I sit still on a lava rock,
a cozy nene cuddles me
in her wonderfully, warm wings, and
curls her downy neck around mine,
like a soft feather lei.

nene (*nay-nay*) — Hawaiian goose

When I am quiet
in Wailea long before lunch,
I hear the plumeria
cascade into the koi pond.

Wailea (*why-lay-ah*)
plumeria (*ploo-mare-ee-ah*) — a fragrant tropical flower

When I sit still in my beach chair,
a baby whale inspires me
with her beginner breeches, and
flaps her fluke above the sea,
like an aloha shaka.

breeches – jumps out of the water
fluke – a whale's tail
shaka (*shaw-kah*) – Hawaiian hang loose hand wave

When I am quiet
in Upcountry Maui right before noon,
I hear the purple blossoms
bloom on the jacaranda tree.

jacaranda (*jack-ah-ran-da*) — a purple flowering tree

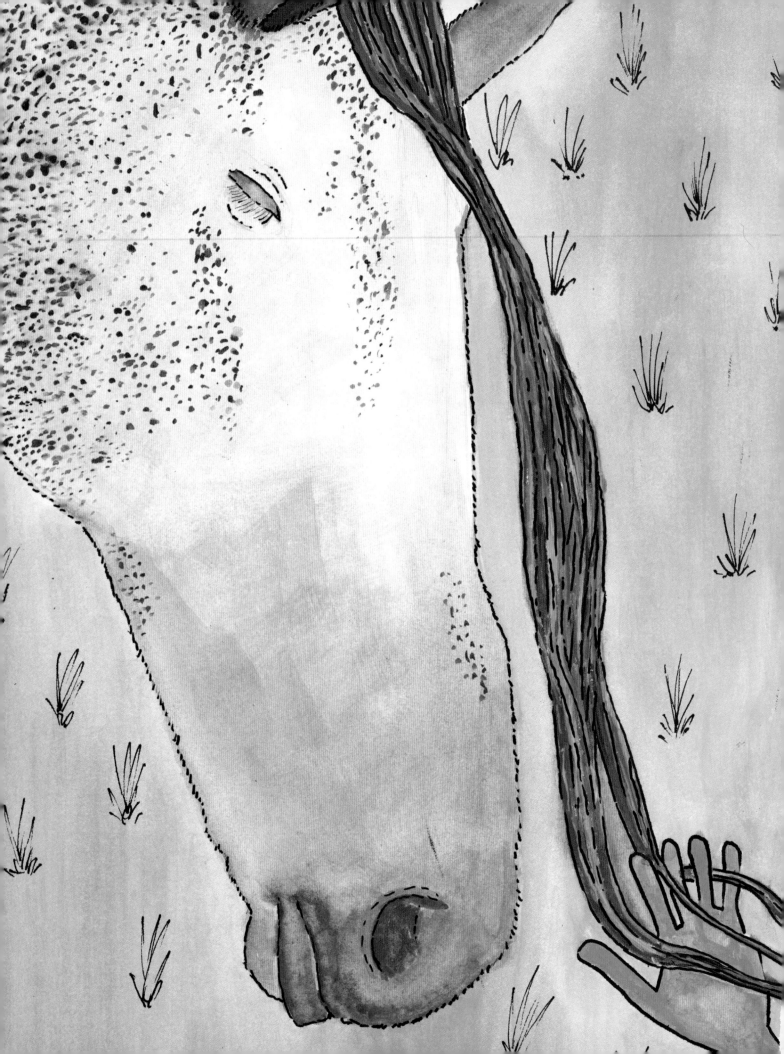

When I stand still in the grass,
a cautious but curious horse nuzzles me,
with his velvety, fuzzy muzzle, and
fans his infinite forelock across my fingers,
like a frayed coconut husk.

When I am quiet
in Paia town at a half past snack time,
I hear the hibiscus
welcome the afternoon tradewinds.

Paia (*Pah-ee-ah*)
hibiscus (*high-bis-cuss*) – the state flower
e komo mai (*ay koh-moh mye*) – welcome

When I stand still by a storefront,
a great dane puppy squashes me
with his over-sized feet, and
kerplunks beside my slippers,
like an exhausted sumo wrestler.

When I am quiet

in Hana Town slightly before three-thirty-three,

I hear the sparkling sunlight

scoot down a mango tree.

Hana (*Hah-nah*)

When I stand still in the bamboo forest,
a mongoose impresses me
with her silent, springy sprints, and
patters her paws across my toes,
like smooth chopsticks in sticky rice.

When I am quiet
at Black Rock long after brunch,
I hear a ukulele's melody
linger on the cliff side.

ukulele (*ooh-koo-lay-lay*) – four stringed instrument

When I stand still in knee-deep water,
a humuhumunukunukuapua'a startles me
with his kaleidoscope of colors, and
flutters his fancy fins near my shins,
like sudsy shampoo ginger.

humuhumunukunukuapua'a (*who-moo-who-moo-noo-koo-noo-koo-ah-poo-ah-ah*) –
Picasso triggerfish (state fish)
shampoo ginger – squeeze its flower to extract fragrant shampoo

When I am quiet
on Tutu's lanai precisely at sunset,
I hear a sleepy jackson yawn
as day melts into night.

Tutu (*Too-too*) – Grandma
lanai (*lah-nye*) – patio
jackson – a type of chameleon

When I lie still on Tutu's pune'e,
a gentle gecko serenades me
with his chirp, chirp, chirp, and
sweeps his tender tail across my chin,
like a sweet butterfly kiss.

gecko – a type of chameleon

pune'e (*poo-nay-ay*) – couch

When I am quiet
in Haiku right around bedtime,
I hear the restless rain
ping, ping, ping on my rusty tin roof.

Haiku (*Hye-koo*)

When I lie still on my bed
a plump pot-bellied pig kisses me
with her perfectly pink lips, and
plops her hefty head on my pillow,
like a hoku nestled in a cloud.

hoku (*hoh-koo*) – star

When you are quiet,
listen to the ʻaina.

When you are still,
what do you feel?

A hui hou kakou.

ʻaina (*eye-nah*) – land, earth
a hui hou kakou (*ah who-ee-ho kah-koh*) – until we meet again

Glossary

(in order of appearance)

Haleakala (*Hah lay ah kah la*) "house of the sun", Maui's dormant volcano

nene (*nay-nay*) — Hawaiian goose

plumeria (*ploo-mare-ee-ah*) — a fragrant tropical flower

breeches — jumps out of the water

fluke — a whale's tail

jacaranda (*jack-ah-ran-da*) — a purple flowering tree

e komo mai (*ay koh-moh mye*) — welcome

humuhumunukunukuapua'a (*who-moo-who-moo-noo-koo-noo-koo-ah-poo-ah-ah*) —
  Picasso triggerfish (state fish)

Tutu (*Too-too*) — Grandma

lanai (*lah-nye*) — patio

jackson — a type of chameleon

gecko — a type of chameleon

pune'e (*poo-nay-ay*) — couch

hoku (*hoh-koo*) — star

'aina (*eye-nah*) — land, earth

a hui hou kakou (*ah who-ee-ho kah-koh*) — until we meet again